SKUNKS FOR BREAKFAST

based on a true story

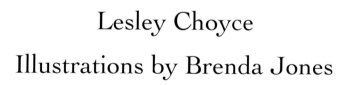

Lesley Choyce

Illustrations by Brenda Jones

NIMBUS
PUBLISHING

Nimbus Publishing Limited
PO Box 9166
Halifax, NS   B3K 5M8
(902) 455-4286

Printed and bound in Canada

Design: Heather Bryan

Library and Archives Canada Cataloguing in Publication

Choyce, Lesley, 1951-
Skunks for breakfast / Lesley Choyce ; illustrations by Brenda Jones.
ISBN 1-55109-586-6

1. Skunks—Juvenile fiction.   I. Jones, Brenda, 1953-   II. Title.
PS8555.H668S53 2006   jC813'.54   C2006-904149-0

Canadä   The Canada Council | Le Conseil des Arts
          for the Arts | du Canada

We acknowledge the financial support of the Government of Canada through the Book Publishing Industry Development Program (BPIDP) and the Canada Council, and of the Province of Nova Scotia through the Department of Tourism, Culture and Heritage for our publishing activities.

This book is dedicated to my daughters,
Sunyata and Pamela.

L. C.

My name is Pamela. I live with my mom and dad
and nineteen-year-old sister, Sunyata, in an old house
by the sea in Nova Scotia. There's a crawlspace
under the house and wild animals sometimes wander
in there. Most of the time they just stay down under
the house and don't bother us.

We were a family that got along great with all
the wild animals—right up to the time of
the disaster.

It was early on a very cold February morning when I woke up to this horrible smell. "Yuck!" I yelled. I jumped up out of bed and ran to my parents' room. "What is that?" I screeched.

My mother was holding her nose and looking upset. My father was still trying to sleep. "What?" he asked.

"Can't you smell it?" I asked.

He sat up and sniffed. "I have a cold. I can't smell so good."

"It's a skunk," my mother said. "I heard some noises. I think a stray cat was under the house and got into a fight with a skunk."

"It's disgusting," I said. *Disgusting* is one of my favourite words.

"It was probably protecting itself," my father said in the skunk's defense.

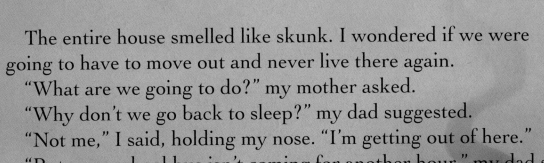

The entire house smelled like skunk. I wondered if we were
going to have to move out and never live there again.

"What are we going to do?" my mother asked.

"Why don't we go back to sleep?" my dad suggested.

"Not me," I said, holding my nose. "I'm getting out of here."

"But your school bus isn't coming for another hour," my dad said.

"I don't care. I'll wait at the end of the road."

I couldn't stand the smell of skunk any longer.

My mother said, "Good. Maybe the wind
will blow some of the stink off." My father
had already fallen back to sleep.

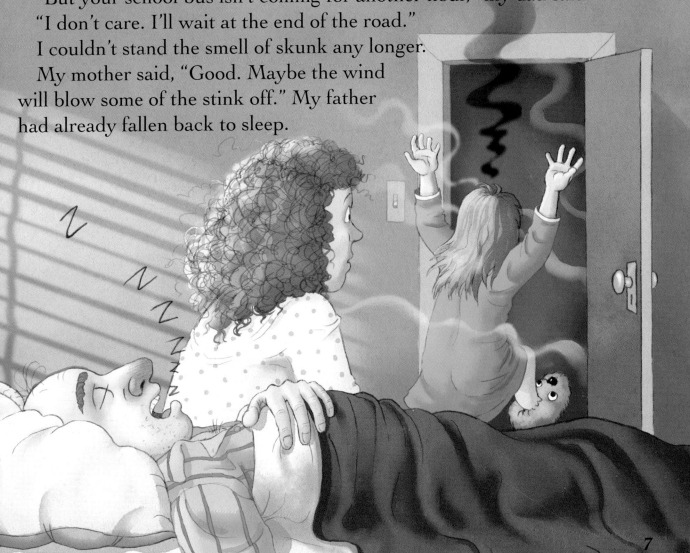

On the bus everybody noticed the smell. I smelled like skunk and all the kids pointed at me. Then they all moved away and I was sitting alone. I felt like crying but I didn't. I tried to pretend that I didn't notice anything was wrong. But it wasn't easy.

At school things only got worse.

When I called my mom from the principal's office to come and pick me up, he had to leave the room because I smelled so bad. Right then I hated skunks and I hated what had happened to me. Why did the skunk pick our house to live under?

Meanwhile, my dad was having his own problems. He had to fly to Toronto that morning. He had already forgotten about the skunk problem as he was walking to his seat on the plane.

People kept looking up from their newspapers and sniffing the air. After he sat down, a man across the aisle asked him, "Do you smell something that smells like…skunk?"

My father said he felt a little guilty. "No," he said. "But I have a cold."

Then everyone on the plane started talking about the skunk smell. So my father read a book and pretended it wasn't him.

The flight attendant went looking for the source of the stink. And so did the co-pilot and eventually the pilot came down the aisle.

The flight was delayed. My father continued to pretend it wasn't him.

Finally, it was decided that the newspapers had been outside and a skunk had been sitting on them. They were taken off the plane and the pilot took off for Toronto.

But I'm sure my father smelled like skunk all day.

When I got home from school, my mom said we should put all the clothes outside and open all the doors and windows. Then we left to visit one of her friends who had a house that didn't smell like skunk.

Soon after, Sunyata arrived home. She had been staying at a friend's house the night of the skunk attack and missed all the excitement.

She saw everyone's clothes thrown on the bushes and in the trees. Some were scattered on the ground. Seeing the back door open, she ran into the kitchen.

13

A note from my mother said, "Get out of the house while you still can." That's when she noticed the horrible smell.

When my dad arrived home the next day, we were all pretty unhappy. Sunyata was watching TV wearing a swimmer's nose plug. I was holed up in my room with my door tightly sealed and tissue paper stuffed up my nose. I kept thinking about the kids laughing at me on the bus. I had decided that I hated skunks and I wanted all the skunks in the world to disappear.

That night, we heard creatures still scratching around under the house. I hid under my covers. When I finally fell asleep, I dreamed there was a skunk in my bedroom. I woke up screaming and my dad came to the rescue. "There's no skunk in your room," he said.

"But there's one under the house and I hate it. It's disgusting."

"I guess something will have to be done," he finally said, yawning.

The next day, I crawled under the house with my dad. We didn't see anything, but it sure did stink.

He hooked up a light and turned on a radio. "The skunks won't like the light and they'll be afraid of the music," he said. He had read this in a book.

But it didn't work.

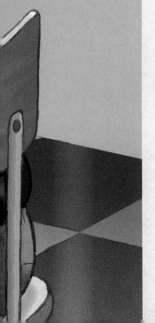

The bad smell was driving us all crazy. And no one would sit near me in school. I sat in the back of the room away from everyone else. My life was ruined. All because of a skunk.

"It could be worse," my father said.

"Don't hurt the skunk," Sunyata said. "Just make him go away."

"What if it's a baby skunk?" I asked. I hated skunks but it didn't seem right to hurt them.

So I went with my father to the hardware store. The man there said, "There are no skunks in Nova Scotia," but our skunk didn't know that. So we bought a trap for catching animals. They went in for the food, a door came down, and they were trapped. But not hurt.

We put fish in the trap on the ground just outside of the house. In the morning, before I even had breakfast, I went to see if it worked.

It had snowed and everything was white. Everything except for the black parts of the skunk caught in the trap. Our troubles were over. Yahoo!

We didn't think it was a good idea to put the skunk in the car so my dad called his friend Glenn, who had a truck. Glenn thought that driving a skunk would be funny and interesting.

My father put on goggles and a white suit that looked like something used for nuclear accidents. When he came close to the cage, the skunk got worried and polluted the front yard as Glenn, Sunyata, and I ran for the bushes. Boy, skunks are really powerful.

After the air cleared, Glenn and my dad drove the skunk to the wilderness to let it go. They had two hockey sticks to open the cage. They took the skunk a long way away because Glenn thought skunks would try to return to their home. Which was our home.

Everybody thought that was the end of the story.

Two nights later we heard more scratching under the house. I woke up and thought it was a nightmare. But it wasn't.

My dad reset the trap. The next morning, he called Glenn. "Guess there were two skunks. You know, like a pair—husband and wife skunks."

My dad got out the white suit and hockey sticks and loaded up another skunk. I thought he was kind of cute. I went along and saw them drop off this skunk at the same place as before. "Wouldn't want to separate a pair of skunks," my father said.

My dad and Glenn smelled really bad and I had to
hold my nose the whole time.

"My girlfriend says my truck smells like skunk,"
Glenn said. "She's not too happy."

When they stopped for coffee, everyone in the shop
squinched up their noses and I couldn't help but laugh.

That night we heard more noises under the house. "What if there's a baby skunk left down there without a mother or father?" I asked.

So the trap was set again.

In the morning, before breakfast, another skunk. This one was smaller and cuter than the rest. I went out and talked to him before my parents woke up. He almost seemed tame.

Then my dad called Glenn and asked another favour.

"This is the last time," Glenn said. "My girlfriend won't ride with me in my truck any more."

News of our skunks spread. Three skunks. What bad luck. But we thought it was over. We decided to reset the trap, "just in case."

Then we caught skunk number four.

Glenn apologized, but said he couldn't help out. He just got a job working on a ship off the coast of Africa.

So I had to help my dad tie the caged skunk onto the top of the station wagon with bungee cords. We took him to join his family.

My sister and I had to keep our clothes outside at night so that we could wear them in the morning. At least it wasn't hard finding a seat by myself on the bus anymore.

A few nights went by without catching anything.

Skunk number five seemed very friendly. I woke up Sunyata and together we fed him raw hot dogs through the wire. "Can we keep him for a pet?" Sunyata asked. But my dad just shook his head as we drove skunk number five to join his family.

Skunk number six was a nervous skunk who didn't like hot dogs. When my dad came out to pick up the cage, the skunk lifted up his tail and my father didn't run fast enough. I laughed and laughed at the expression on his face.

"Looks like it's going to be one of those days," he said.

When people saw us driving down the road each day with a skunk on top, they ran inside their houses.

I read that skunks have litters of ten or eleven babies so I told my dad that I thought skunk number thirteen was the last.

But it didn't work out that way.

There was a heavy snow the morning of skunk number sixteen. We towed the trapped skunk to the car on my sled and my dad tied him on top. Then we headed for the usual place.

The roads were really icy. My dad took a corner too fast. He lost control of the car and he slammed on the brakes. The car skidded off the road and barely missed a line of mailboxes. Then we came to a stop with our front wheels dangling over a steep drop-off with a half-frozen lake below. My heart was beating like crazy.

It was a close call, but we were okay.

And so was the skunk.

After we got the car back on the road, we drove the skunk to join his family. When we opened the cage with the hockey stick, the skunk ran for the woods but then turned and looked back at us as if he was saying good-bye. I felt a little sad because I had learned to like the skunks, even if they were incredibly stinky.

And that was the last we saw of them. From now on, there'll be no more skunks for breakfast.